A Note to Parents and Caregivers:

Read-it! Readers are for children who are just starting on the amazing road to reading. These beautiful books support both the acquisition of reading skills and the love of books.

The PURPLE LEVEL presents basic topics and objects using high frequency words and simple language patterns.

The RED LEVEL presents familiar topics using common words and repeating sentence patterns.

The BLUE LEVEL presents new ideas using a larger vocabulary and varied sentence structure.

The YELLOW LEVEL presents more challenging ideas, a broad vocabulary, and wide variety in sentence structure.

The GREEN LEVEL presents more complex ideas, an extended vocabulary range, and expanded language structures.

The ORANGE LEVEL presents a wide range of ideas and concepts using challenging vocabulary and complex language structures.

When sharing a book with your child, read in short stretches, pausing often to talk about the pictures. Have your child turn the pages and point to the pictures and familiar words. And be sure to reread favorite stories or parts of stories.

There is no right or wrong way to share books with children. Find time to read with your child, and pass on the legacy of literacy.

Adria F. Klein, Ph.D.
Professor Emeritus
California State University
San Bernardino, California

Editor: Patricia Stockland
Page Production: Amy Bailey Muehlenhardt/JoAnne Nelson/Tracy Davies
Art Director: Keith Griffin
Managing Editor: Catherine Neitge
The illustrations in this book were rendered digitally.

Picture Window Books
5115 Excelsior Boulevard
Suite 232
Minneapolis, MN 55416
877-845-8392
www.picturewindowbooks.com

Printed in the United States of America.

Library of Congress Cataloging-in-Publication Data
Blair, Eric.
Johnny Appleseed / by Eric Blair ; illustrated by Amy Bailey Muehlenhardt.
p. cm. — (Read-it! readers tall tales)
Summary: Relates episodes from the life of Johnny Appleseed, a peaceful man who
roamed the West for fifty years planting and tending to the trees that bore his favorite
fruit, the apple.
ISBN 1-4048-0971-6 (hardcover)
1. Appleseed, Johnny, 1774-1845—Juvenile literature. 2. Apple growers—United
States—Biography—Juvenile literature. 3. Frontier and pioneer life—Middle West—
Juvenile literature. [1. Appleseed, Johnny, 1774-1845. 2. Apple growers. 3. Frontier
and pioneer life.] I. Muehlenhardt, Amy Bailey, 1974- ill. II. Title. III. Series: Read-it!
readers tall tales.
SB63.C46B59 2004
634.11'092—dc22
2004018433

Johnny Appleseed

By Eric Blair
Illustrated by Amy Bailey Muehlenhardt

Special thanks to our advisers for their expertise:

Adria F. Klein, Ph.D.
Professor Emeritus, California State University
San Bernardino, California

Susan Kesselring, M.A.
Literacy Educator
Rosemount-Apple Valley-Eagan (Minnesota) School District

PICTURE WINDOW BOOKS
Minneapolis, Minnesota

When Johnny Appleseed was a young boy, he loved apples and apple trees.

CHILDREN'S ROOM

5

He loved the way apples looked.

He loved the way
apples smelled.

7

Most of all, he loved the way the juicy apples tasted.

As Johnny grew up, he became tall and thin. He always wore a very big smile. He carried a cooking pot on his head for his travels.

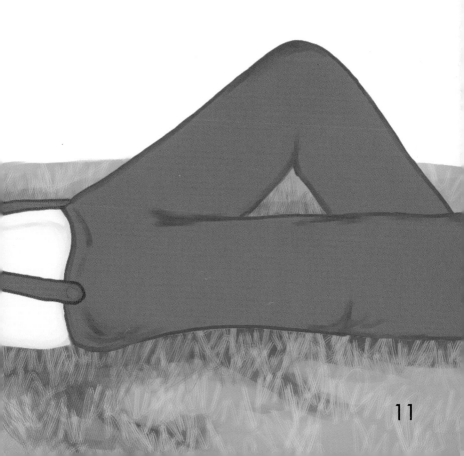

When he was old enough to leave home, Johnny became an explorer.

13

Johnny was no regular explorer, though. He didn't carry a gun or weapon.

Instead, Johnny always carried a sack of apple seeds with him.

Johnny wanted other people to enjoy apple trees as much as he did.

So, he roamed around until he found good places to plant the seeds.

When he found a good place, Johnny would clear and prepare the land.

Then he would plant the apple
seeds in neat rows.

As the apple trees grew, Johnny
would sell them or give them
to settlers.

The settlers loved Johnny's visits.

He always told good stories.

Johnny had many stories to tell.

Johnny roamed the West for fifty
years. During his travels, he had
many adventures.

Johnny always walked barefoot through the wilderness. Once, a rattlesnake bit the sole of his foot. But his feet were so tough that the fangs didn't break the skin.

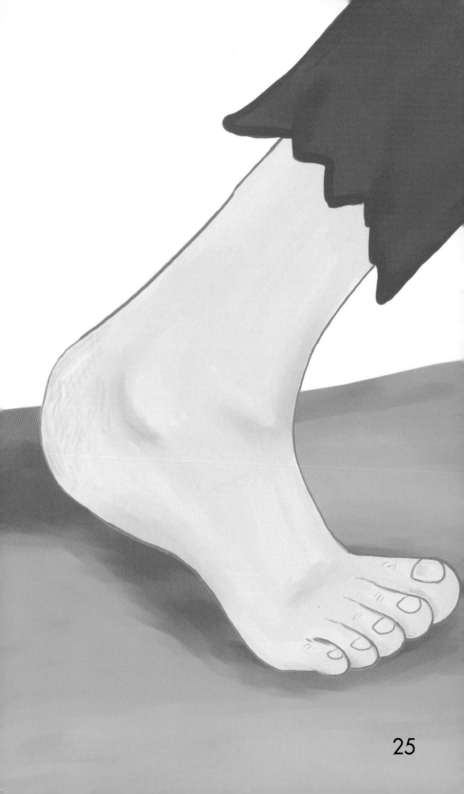

25

Johnny could talk to all the animals.
One day, he rescued a wolf from
a trap.

After he talked to the wolf, it became his best friend.

Johnny also became friends with the Indians.

They enjoyed his stories and
apples, too.

After years of planting trees, Johnny had friends across the country.

he wilderness was no longer so wild,
hanks to Johnny's apple seeds and
is friendly smile.

31

More *Read-it!* Readers

Bright pictures and fun stories help you practice your reading skills. Look for more books at your level.

TALL TALES

Annie Oakley, Sharp Shooter by Eric Blair

John Henry by Christianne C. Jones

Johnny Appleseed by Eric Blair

The Legend of Daniel Boone by Eric Blair

Paul Bunyan by Eric Blair

Pecos Bill by Eric Blair

Looking for a specific title or level? A complete list of *Read-it!* Readers is available on our Web site: *www.picturewindowbooks.com*